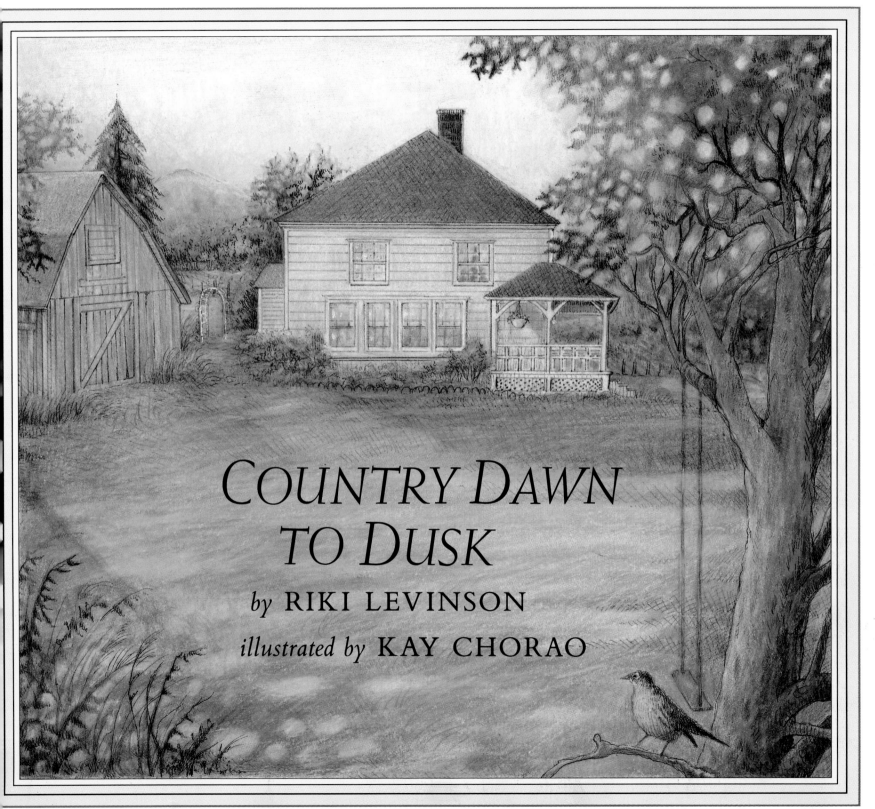

COUNTRY DAWN TO DUSK

by RIKI LEVINSON

illustrated by KAY CHORAO

DUTTON CHILDREN'S BOOKS   NEW YORK

to Gerry, my one and only
—R.L.

to Barbara Moore and
the children of Laurel School
—K.C.

Text copyright © 1992 by Riki Friedberg Levinson
Illustrations copyright © 1992 by Kay Sproat Chorao

Library of Congress Cataloging-in-Publication Data

Levinson, Riki.
Country Dawn to Dusk / by Riki Levinson;
illustrated by Kay Chorao.—1st ed.
p.   cm.
Summary: A girl and her dog go through a day highlighted by
the vivid colors of sunrise, rain, mountains, forests, a rainbow,
and sunset.
ISBN 0-525-44957-4
[1. Country life—Fiction.] I. Chorao, Kay, ill. II. Title.
PZ7.L5796Cou   1992
[E]—dc20   91-34600   CIP   AC

Published in the United States by Dutton Children's Books,
a division of Penguin Books USA Inc.
375 Hudson Street, New York, New York 10014

Designer: Riki Levinson

Printed in Hong Kong by South China Printing Co.
First Edition   10 9 8 7 6 5 4 3 2 1

Early in the morning, I hear the dogs barking.

I look out the window and see my father playing with them.

My dog, Barker, jumps the highest and catches the stick.

The sky shines pink on the pond below the hill.

Quickly, I get out of bed and dress. It is very cold.

I look out again, but my father and the dogs are gone.

The deep orange sun peeks over the edge of the hill.

I race downstairs to eat. Barker and I want to
play together before the school bus comes.
Mother gives me oatmeal to make me warm.
I eat too quickly and burn my tongue.

I grab my jacket and run outside. Barker is waiting.
I pick up a stick and toss it into the air.
Barker jumps high to catch it.
The golden sun is up above the hill.

The school bus comes and waits for me on the road.
Barker runs with me. He barks and barks as I hop onto
the bus. All the children laugh when I bark back.

We ride through forests of black trees and white trees.
Then down, down, down the turning road,
past snow-topped mountains trimmed with green,
then past the village grocery by the lake, to school.

We jump off the bus and run through the wind
to the schoolhouse.

I hang up my jacket and go to my seat.
I can hear the wind while we learn to read.

After we finish our lessons, we sing.
I can still hear the wind. It pushes harder,
rattling the windowpanes.
I look out.
Grey clouds sweep across the sky over the lake.

It's time to play games, but I want to stay by the window.
I put my hand on the glass and feel the wet cold.
Heavy rains slap the ground, then lift and swirl,
round and round.

Swiftly, the wind hurries the dark sky away.

And suddenly, the rain stops.

A beautiful rainbow touches the lake.

Finally, school is over.

We race outside and get on the bus to go home.

First we pass the village stores,

then up, up, up the turning road,

past snow-topped mountains trimmed with green.

We ride through forests of black trees and white trees.

I watch for Barker. He's waiting for me.

He barks and barks to say hello.

All the children laugh when I bark back.

I pick up a stick and toss it high into the air.

Barker runs to catch it.

It's too cold. Barker and I hurry into the house.

Mother gives me hot cocoa to make me warm.

I look out the window as I sip it.

The deep orange sun sinks slowly down,

then drops behind the trees.

And suddenly, the sun is gone.

Father comes in, closing the door quickly
to keep out the cold.
We sit together by the fire.
Barker curls up at our feet.

Later, Mother puts supper on the table.
I look out the window as we eat.
The dark blue sky, edged with pink,
shines through the trees beyond the field.